Under the Ramadan Moon

Sylvia Whitman   Illustrated by Sue Williams

Albert Whitman & Company, Chicago, Illinois

To Majida and Munir, of course, and the littlest ones: Ahmed, Aichoucha, Khadija, Kmar, Meriem, Omar, and Youssef—Sʏʟᴠɪᴀ

For the twins, Lilly and Jack, with love—Sᴜᴇ

Special thanks to Habeeb Quadri, Principal, Muslim Community Center Full Time School, Morton Grove, Illinois.

Library of Congress Cataloging-in-Publication Data

Whitman, Sylvia
Under the Ramadan moon / by Sylvia Whitman ; illustrated by Sue Williams.
p.   cm.
1. Ramadan—Juvenile literature. 2. Facts and feasts—Islam—Juvenile literature. I Williams, Sue. ill. II. Title.
BP186.4.W46 2008 297.3'62—dc22 2008001307

Text copyright © 2008 by Sylvia Whitman
Illustrations copyright © 2008 by Sue Williams
Published in 2008 by Albert Whitman & Company
ISBN 978-0-8075-8305-0

Printed in China
10 9 8 7 6 5 NP 20 19 18 17 16

Design by Carol Gildar

For more information about Albert Whitman & Company, visit our web site at www.albertwhitman.com.

We wait for the moon.
We watch for the moon.
We watch for the Ramadan moon.

We fast by day
under the moon,
under the moon,
under the Ramadan moon.

We eat at night
under the moon,
under the moon,
under the Ramadan moon.

**We speak kind words
and stop bad habits
under the moon.**

We give to the poor
and read Qur'an
under the moon.

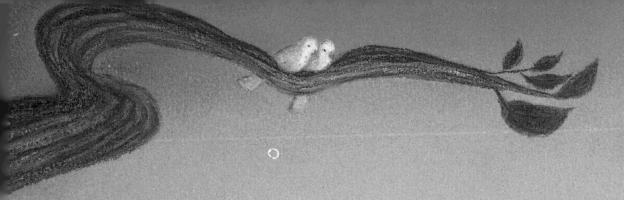

We hang bright lights
 and bake sweet treats
  under the Ramadan moon.

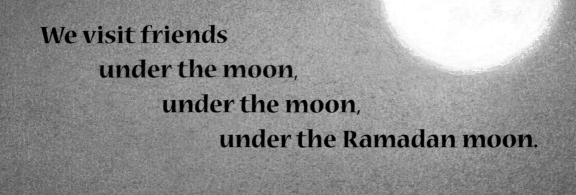

We visit friends
    under the moon,
        under the moon,
            under the Ramadan moon.

We crack nuts
    and drink hot tea
        under the moon.

We tell stories
 and laugh and play
  under the moon.

Then together we pray
under the moon,
under the moon,
under the Ramadan moon.

We live our faith
  until next year
    under the moon,
      under the moon,
        under the Ramadan moon.

About Ramadan

Ramadan is a time for serious reflection and happy celebration for Muslims. It is the ninth—and most special—month in the religious year. Since the Islamic calendar measures months by moon cycles, the date of Ramadan changes gradually over time. But no matter the season, Ramadan always begins with the crescent of a new moon.

During Ramadan, most Muslims fast during the day: we do not eat or drink. We wake up before the sun rises for a meal called *suhoor,* and when there is enough day-light to tell a white thread from a black one, we begin our fast. All adult Muslims are expected to fast—although not all do—unless they are sick, pregnant, or traveling. Children practice with short fasts until they are ready for the full day, usually as teenagers. We go to work and school as usual while we fast.

By fasting, believers build self-control. We "clean up our act" in other ways, too. Some people quit smoking. Others stop getting angry. Fasting is a way to purify our bodies and turn our minds toward God. Hunger also reminds us of the suffering of the poor. Islam requires believers to donate a share of their wealth to the needy every year, and many Muslims give during Ramadan.

Prayer is another important part of Ramadan. Muslims usually pray five times a day, but we often pray more during this time of year. We go to the mosque, and we read aloud from the Qur'an, the holy book of Islam. Some Muslims recite the whole Arabic text—more than six thousand verses—over the course of Ramadan.

Although Ramadan is demanding, it is also fun. As soon as the sun sets, families sit down to *iftar,* the fast-breaking meal. We enjoy special soups and breads as well as pastries stuffed with sweet cheese or nuts. Friends and family visit and snack long into the evening. In the United States, Ramadan recipes and customs reflect the many different cultures Muslim Americans come from. Under the moon we share holiday foods, games, and traditions.

Ramadan ends just as it began, with a new moon. A three-day holiday follows— Eid al-Fitr, the Feast of Fast Breaking. Joyful Muslims gather in enormous groups for the first Eid prayer.

Dressed in new clothes, we host friends and family at home and exchange presents for children. We thank God for all our blessings—especially the strength to fast and pray.

—Sylvia Whitman